The Island of Monsters

by

Noah F. Bunyan

Prologue

Atlantis (1600 B.C.)

The Energy Crystal glowed at full power and it could be seen for miles across the ocean. Two armies battled at the gates of Atlantis. As the crystal continued to build up power, the attackers fought a losing battle against hundreds of Atlanteans and unimaginably horrible monsters. The crystal grew brighter and brighter until a beam of pure energy shot out of it and across the ocean. The beam destroyed everything in its path.

A lone warrior raised his bow and fired at the crystal on the palace roof. The arrow hit between the gears of a colossal machine and the tower buckled and after a moment, it crumbled to the ground. The force of the explosion destroyed their entire palace and the earth shook from the force of the explosion. People ran as the earth crumbled beneath their feet. As the island sank into the ocean, many boats sailed away. On one of the boats stood the man who was once this island's king. As his guards paddled the boat, below deck he looked out at his sinking kingdom. He knew that someday, revenge would be his.

1945

A small deserted island in the Pacific

His boat rocked back and forth. He had searched for this island for many years and now it was just beyond the horizon. He had spent months researching the strange stories sailors told about the island. He spent even longer sailing through the ocean during storms and through turbulent seas, trying to find the island's location. Now, at last, he was here. "With the crystals on this island, I will change the world," he thought.

Chapter 1

Now

Somewhere over the Pacific Ocean

The plane shook violently. The intercom came on and the pilot announced, "We're going through a bit of turbulence. Please fasten your seatbelts."

Max began to fasten his seatbelt when he heard a man's voice near the back of the plane, "Do you wish you had better hair? You must try my new hair care product, Shamfroo!" Then came the voice of a flight attendant, "Sir, sit down please." Max thought back to how he came to be in this small plane in the middle of the Atlantic in a thunderstorm. For years, he tried to get his book about the lost city of Atlantis published and after dozens of failures, a company in Japan offered to publish his book if he met with them in person, so he was flying out to meet with them.

Suddenly, he heard the loud roar of thunder and the plane shook, waking him from his thoughts. He looked out the window as lightning flashed around them. A bolt of lightning struck the wing of the plane. He heard other passengers gasping as the attendants announced they would need to make an emergency landing. People screamed as bottles of shampoo flew past them, splattering on the walls of the plane. Oxygen masks dropped from above him and the lights flickered off and on. Max tried not to blackout, but he lost consciousness as the plane descended rapidly.

Timmy poked the unconscious man lying on the raft. The man had been asleep since the plane came down an hour ago. The co-pilot said, "Hey kid, get away from him!" The boy backed away as one of the passengers, maybe it was the man who'd been talking about haircare products earlier, shouted, "Look, an island!" The other passengers began paddling. Timmy was a young boy, only eight years-old with brown hair. He was taking the plane to Beijing to compete in the World Spelling Bee Olympics.

Another passenger on the downed plane, Randon, was a 32 year-old man with dark skin and an afro. He just wore sweatpants and a t-shirt and was rather skinny. He had invented a new kind of haircare product which he called Shamfroo. Unfortunately, he had not sold a single bottle for over a year, but he was persistent and would not give up. He had decided to go to Tokyo and sell it there, as it was the only place he hadn't tried to sell it. Last year, he was chased out of Antarctica by angry penguins. Randon looked across the sea. What he saw lifted his spirits which made him yell, "Look, an island!"

"This could not be happening to him. Not now" he thought. He was close to finally escaping from the police who he had hidden from for years, but now the plane he was in had crashed. He shouldn't have tried to save time by taking a plane. He should have hidden away on a boat instead. Now he would never get to France! He hid the money in his briefcase but it would only be a matter of time before someone found out.

Chapter 2

The rubber raft hit the sand of the island. As the passengers pulled the boat to shore, Max woke up to the sound of a Golden Retriever barking in his ears. The dog belonged to another passenger. A flight attendant had helped it out of the cargo hold after the plane went down. The dog ran off the raft and onto the beach, wagging his tail. Max walked over to the pilot, who was busy trying to fix the radio and send a message. He didn't realize it yet, but the radio had been damaged beyond repair and even if it hadn't been, the radio could not work on *this island.*

"Where are we, what happened?" Max's question interrupted the pilot from his work.

"It's you, the knocked out guy, isn't it?" replied the pilot. I don't know where we are, the plane crashed and none of our devices seem to be working."

"Did anyone get hurt?" asked Max.

The pilot answered, "A few bruises and someone got shampoo in their eyes. I need to get back to work. Can you calm that woman over there down?" A woman further down the beach was sitting and repeating to herself, "It crashed, it crashed, the plane crashed!" and waving her hands in the air.

"After you've calmed her down, I'd like you and a few others to see if this island has any people on it," the pilot said to him, as Max walked towards the woman.

It watched from the shadows silently. It was the perfect hunter on this island but the prey it saw now was strange. Similar to the ones who lived in caves, but different somehow. It was the king of the jungle and could watch its prey as long as it wanted, stalking it until it decided to attack.

They walked through the dense jungle. It was hot and humid and the air felt like it weighed a million tons. There were trees, vines, leaves, and noises that made it difficult to explore. Max, Randon, and a muscular bald man named Mark looked for signs of others. So far, they'd seen nothing except some kind of iguana-like lizard with spikes on its back. There were lots of noises.

"We should look by those mountains over there and get out of this jungle, we can't find anything in here," said Max. So the group turned to the right and continued their trip. Randon started to tell Max about his Shamfroo. He was saying his Shamfroo was better than any other product when all of the sudden, a creature exploded through the bushes knocking, big Mark to the ground. The creature kept running and then disappeared back into the jungle through the bushes.

"What was that thing!?" yelled Randon.

"I think it was a wild boar," Max yelled back to him.

Mark got up from the jungle floor and brushed himself off. He looked through the forest and at the hoof tracks on the ground. He rubbed his leg where the creature had hit him and replied to Max, "That thing was no wild boar, it was a monster!"

Chapter 3

Max couldn't believe it, a day ago he had been about to go to Japan to publish a book, now he was on a deserted island in the middle of the ocean. Who knew how long he would be there before someone rescued him. He sat near the fire on the beach with the other passengers. The Golden Retriever lay near the bamboo shelter they had built. Others were eating bananas from a banana tree further down the beach. The dog suddenly woke and started barking at the jungle, trying to break out of its leash. The dog's owner, Alice, ran to calm the dog. "Ruffus, quiet, stop barking! What's a matter with you?"

Ruffus continued to bark and stretch its leash further towards the jungle. The dog barked louder and louder until a terrifying sound came from the jungle. It was the sound of a predator, the sound of a hunter. Max and the others on the beach were frozen in fear. The dog whimpered and ran towards the people at the fire, away from the jungle. They all heard the creature backing away and moving further into the forest. After it left, the plane passengers sat there for a minute, before Mark got up and broke the silence, "Like I said before, it's a monster!"

1946 June 15

The journal of Dr. Ethan White

I have been on this island for over a year now. My experiments are becoming increasingly successful. I am close to cracking the secret of the crystals through my experiments. Soon, I may need to leave this island and return to Europe. The natives of the island continue to attack my lab. They demand that I leave. I know if I do not leave, soon they will attack.

The animals are getting restless in their cages. I must stop writing.

Now

The people on the beach were afraid and it was difficult to sleep that night. It seemed the island hid strange creatures from them. The noises were frightening. The pilot, a man named Robert and his co-pilot Joe could not fix the radio. If they could not contact anyone, who knew how long it would be until they were rescued? What if no one ever found them?

It was decided that the co-pilot would lead a group to the top of a small nearby mountain. He would stay there to keep a fire going for two days, and then switch with someone. Hopefully, if a plane passed, they would see the fire. The people he chose to set up the fire were Mark, Randon and Alice. They began the journey at noon and entered the mysterious and frightening jungle.

Chapter 4

What had he found? Timmy had just been going for a walk down to the beach when he nearly stepped on it. He yelled to the nearby flight attendants and everyone came running. The creature was dead. It was a snake, bigger than a python but with spikes all over its back. The crowd gathered around it. The flight attendant tried to get them to stay calm. After a few moments, they began to talk amongst themselves. "What if this snake-like creature had gotten into our camp? We have to protect ourselves. The monster from last night was bigger than this. We have to get off this island!"

Joe felt he was being watched the whole time he climbed the mountain. He acted brave but what happened the night before had scared him. The others left an hour ago. Now, he watched the fire alone. There it was again, the feeling that he was being watched. He looked out to a nearby mountain, bigger than the one he was on. He looked up to its peak and squinted. It wasn't clear but he thought he saw…. no it couldn't be. He laughed to himself and sat down. His mind was playing tricks on him. He couldn't believe it, but maybe he was right. He yelled to the others as loud as he could, but they were already gone.

Back at the beach, fellow passengers were talking about the snake-like creature. Phillip, who was a doctor, knew the snake was dead but it scared him nonetheless.

He had said himself, "What was this place? Monster Island." This couldn't be possible. He had to get off the island. It would only be a matter of time before they found the briefcase that had millions of dollars in it. He could not be stuck living some low-budget monster movie. He had to get out of here before they learned who he really was. His disguise would not work much longer.

Randon could not wait to get back to the beach. The jungle scared him. The thing that attacked Mark scared him. "What's next, King Kong?" he thought to himself. He was so scared he stopped trying to sell Shamfroo to Mark and Alice. He thought about it though, why it was that saying "I use Shamfroo and look at my hair" did not seem to work? "I have great hair. Everyone should want this Shamfroo," he thought.

Chapter 5

Phillip awoke and got up from the sand he laid on. The team in charge of the project had not yet finished the second bamboo shack. He looked up at the mountains and the smoke he was used to seeing each day after a week on the island was gone? "The fire is out!" he yelled, waking everyone.

Max, Mark, Alice, and Phillip ran through the jungle. They had gone a few days without problems and the castaways had calmed down, but now, they were back to hysteria. Randon had been on the mountain monitoring the fire the night before. "What could have happened to him?" said Max.

As they climbed the mountain they heard strange sounds like a bird chirping but deeper and louder. Soon, they reached the top of the mountain and found that Randon was gone. The fire had died long ago and the wood was cold. Max looked on the ground and found Randon's footprints leading away from the camp down the mountain. "Look!" Max yelled.

"Why would he leave the fire?" said Phillip.

"Wait, there are more footprints. These aren't Randon's!" said Alice. Max looked at the trail of footprints. It seemed Randon and two others had left the camp. They walked down the mountain into a mysterious canyon below.

The hunter watched its prey climb into the canyon. It prepared to pounce but stopped. The canyon was dangerous. The hunter would enter if it was desperate for food but it was not hungry. The other creatures could have the prey walking into the canyon. There was plenty more on the beach.

Mark led the way through the canyon. It had been a steep walk down the mountain and they had nearly lost the footprints twice. He wasn't sure who or what the tracks belonged to but would find out soon enough. He looked up at the hot sun and then back down at the tracks when suddenly a shadow passed over them and they heard, "Shreeek! Shreeeeek!"

"What is that?" asked Alice.

The shadow passed over them again and Mark yelled, "Run, head for that cave!" He looked up as it flew closer. "It's going to land!" They ran into the cave just as huge talons hit the ground.

"Are we safe now?" asked Alice.

Max replied, "I think so," just as dust fell from the cave roof, as if something was climbing above them.

Phillip walked deeper into the cave and yelled to Mark, pointing "What's that back there?"

Mark went over to see what Phillip was talking about and found that the back of the cave was filled with glowing yellow crystals. "This is amazing!" Mark said. "We could sell these and make millions when we get off this island."

"No, you cannot!" said a deep voice from behind them. "The crystals are ours!"

Chapter 6

22nd June 1946

The journal of Dr. Ethan White

The natives have informed me they will put up with my presence no longer but I cannot leave yet. I am so close to success. The panther cub I used the formula on is my most successful experiment yet.

I have just heard a crash. It sounds like the natives are trying to break into my lab! I must stop them.

Now

It was late at night and the other castaways were asleep. He finished filling in the hole he had dug and looked back to the camp. When help finally came, he would dig up the briefcase along with the millions inside. Suddenly, he froze. Someone was coming. He hid behind a sand dune as two figures walked out of the forest. It was two of the people who went to check why the fire stopped, Max and the girl whose name he could not remember. Annie? Alexis? He wondered where the other two who were with them had gone. They walked down the beach towards the huts that the castaways slept in. He took one more look at the hole he had dug, then began to walk back to find out what was going on.

Everyone was awake now and surrounded Max and Alice. As they began to quiet down, Max spoke, "We went up to the mountain top but Randon was missing. There were also two other footprints besides his leading into the canyon at the base of the mountain." Alice added, "We were attacked by a creature, then Phillip and Mark disappeared. We think whoever or whatever took Randon also got them."

Someone yelled, "Look up at the mountains!" A beam of light was slowly moving down the mountainside and through the jungle. "They're coming for us!"

Phillip sat in the dark cell. Who were these people? Why have they taken us to these underground tunnels deep inside the cave? What was going on? He looked at the guard in front of his cell. He wore some sort of tunic and held a spear with one of the crystals from the cave as its tip. He also wore a headband with a crystal on it in front of his forehead. He was bald and his eyes were large with no pupils. They seemed to glow in the darkness of the tunnel.

Phillip tried to speak to the man, "Can I have some water?" The guard looked back but did not reply. Another of the men walked down the tunnel. He looked like the guard but wore crystal wristbands and a crystal necklace. Phillip stared at the guard without speaking. The guard seemed to reply to the other man in what sounded like Latin or Greek and then walked away. As the other man took the guard's place, Phillip thought, "What is going to happen to them?"

Chapter 7

Robert, the plane's captain, yelled for everyone to grab whatever they could carry. "I don't know what those lights are but I don't want to be here when they get to the beach," he said. As everyone looked around and grabbed whatever they could, the Golden Retriever ran alarmingly around them barking loudly.

"Are you sure we should go?" someone said as they walked into the jungle, not knowing they were being watched.

As they trekked into the jungle no one was sure what they would find when they returned to the beach. Max looked into the dense jungle. He saw something move by fast through the bushes to their right. He didn't see it clearly but it was small and moved quickly. He thought to himself, "Will we ever get off this island?"

He looked up to see a bright amber light coming towards them fast. He yelled, "Run!" The castaways frantically started to run but a net flew out of the trees knocking Captain Robert to the ground. Nets continued to fly in all directions. Three had already been captured. Max and the others continued running. Max felt tired but the fright and adrenaline kept him going.

They stayed together, running on and on as the trees began to thin. They stopped and grouped together. The forest had disappeared and ahead they saw a small rocky beach. The captain, co-pilot and one flight attendant were missing, seemingly captured. Max began to notice strange markings on the trees they passed by them in the jungle. Huge claw marks, like from a Bengal tiger, or a grizzly bear. Max couldn't imagine what sort of monster had made them. He turned away and realized he had strayed from the group. He ran back up to them and took one last look at the claw marks. Up ahead the trees thinned out more and more until suddenly, Timmy yelled, "Look, a lake and there's a boat!"

Phillip had been planning how to get out of his cell all night and was finally ready. Soon he would get out of here and finally learn what was going on. The guard watching him looked away. Perfect, he would begin the escape now!

Max, Alice, Timmy, Ruffus the dog, two flight attendants, a man in a suit named Jack, and the woman named Martha were all that were left of the castaways. They walked slowly alongside the lake, moving closer and closer to the boat on the other side. It looked like an old fishing boat with rusty broken portholes on the sides. It was about thirty feet long and abandoned. Max decided to climb aboard.

Alice wondered who had been throwing those nets the night before and where had the others disappeared to? Were there others on the island and if so, what did they want?

Max walked through the boat searching for clues to where it had come from. Everything on the boat was in bad condition, broken, and covered in spider webs. He brushed a web out of his way and opened a rusty cabinet door inside a small room that looked like the captain's cabin. There was a torn and yellowing document, a map. It was still readable and showed the Pacific Ocean. In the center of the ocean was a small 'x' with the words 'The Island of Monsters' next to it.

Chapter 8

When Max climbed down from the boat, he yelled "Look what I found," holding the map up. As he turned, the only one standing there was Jack. "Where is everyone?" Max asked.

Jack said, "Calm down. That kid, Timmy, found a stone path over there leading into the jungle. They told me to wait for you and then meet up with them.

Max said they have to see this map, so he and Jack followed the path. Max asked, "Why were you on the plane?"

Jack replied, "I'm CEO of a business back in America. I was heading to Japan to climb Mt. Fuji while on vacation."

What does your business do?" Max asked.

"We mostly sell cars and film TV shows. We do some other stuff too," replied Jack.

Phillip ran through the tunnels. His escape plan had not gone as well as he thought it would but he got out. Dozens of guards chased after him but there was something else in here, something big. "Where was the exit, how can I get free?" he thought. He looked to his right and saw a faint light. Was it the exit? He heard a loud roar behind him. He tried to run faster but his sides hurt and he was running out of breath. He ran closer to the light. He was almost to it but the army of men, each with a crystal spear and headband, closed in on him.

The creature jumped towards him. It was huge and took up most of the tunnel. It was like a bear but with gigantic claws and a strange scorpion-like tail. What was it? It had a crystal headband on its head, just like the guards. He had to get out of here. He dived towards the light, just missing the bear-like creature. It was an exit, and he ran out of the tunnel.

He looked around quickly and saw the others were still behind him. He expected to be back in the dense jungle but instead he saw he had not escaped at all. He was in a huge cavern and far below was molten lava. He was on a high cliff-like path. At the end was long narrow bridge leading to a huge building. It was a castle made of black lava rock rising out of lava. There were bridges spread out from the castle leading to other exits from the cavern. On all of the bridges were more bear-like scorpion creatures. They were pulling carts driven by more of the bald crystal-wearing cave people. The yellow crystals glowed. Suddenly, he heard the other cave people behind him. He was trapped.

Jack and Max reached the end of the stone path and there was a steel-like building at the end of the path on the edge of a mountain. They didn't see the others. They ran up to the building, all the windows were broken and the door was hanging off its hinges. There was barbed wire all around the building but most had fallen away with time. Max yelled out, "Hellooooo, is anybody there?"

He heard Timmy yell from inside, "We're in here, Max!"

Relieved, Max entered the building with Jack close behind. They entered a room full of knocked over tables and drawers. On the floor were broken cups, crashed beakers, broken slides, and two microscopes. Dirt was all over the floor and ivy crept up the walls. Huge spider webs went from floor to ceiling all over the room. Jack looked at the others and said, "I wonder how big the spiders are?" They passed by several large unlocked cages. It was strange. They walked into another room and an old desk of rotting wood sat to the side. Timmy lifted an old book off the desk. It was moldy with torn pages. It looked like it had not been opened in years. The cover was faded but Max could read it. It said "The Journal of Dr. Ethan White."

"What is this?" Max asked.

"Open it," replied Timmy.

Chapter 9

The sun had set and the castaways were resting inside the building they had found. Max and Timmy were studying the journal. The pages were mostly unreadable but a bit could be deciphered. Timmy read some to the group. They found that Dr. Ethan White had been a scientist researching crystals found only on this island. When melted down, the crystals had power, they could mutate creatures. Looking at the dates in the journal, in 1945, Dr. White had spent over a year on this island testing different amounts on the wildlife. He wrote about natives and his scientific experiments.

Max showed the others the map from the boat but it was dated 1941? The journal entries explained the creature Max had seen but there were two things he didn't understand. The map and boat were from four years before Dr. White had come to the island? Were the natives he wrote about the ones who were kidnapping the castaways? Suddenly, they heard a sound outside. Max jumped up and peered through a broken window. He looked into the darkness of the jungle but saw nothing. He turned around when a huge jet-black shape flew out of the jungle and ran toward the building. Its clawed hand broke through the window.

Timmy ran to a back room and frantically brushed a web out of the way. "That's weird." On the floor was a large pit, what could it be? He heard something move. A large spider, the size of his head, came jumping out. Timmy screamed with horror. More spiders were crawling out of the pit. He ran back to Max. The huge claw was still crashing through the window. It scraped against the walls, leaving marks on the steel. Max yelled and fell backwards. All the castaways ran back to the room with the spiders. They were crawling all over the place.

Somebody yelled, "Get outside!"

Alice yelled, "No way, the claw!"

Max thought, are we trapped, will we die?

It crawled up the tunnel surrounded by the spiders. "Hummanns here. Hummanns in my place. Hummmmmm." It began climbing faster.

Max tried to think of a way to get everyone to safety. They were trapped between the creature with the claws and basketball-sized spiders that could be venomous. Max noticed that the spiders were all moving to the sides of the room as if clearing a path. Jack ran at the path, trying to get out but as he did, several spiders jumped and knocked him back. Then a hideous creature crawled out of the pit.

28

It was grey with rags that may have once been clothes. It stood on two long, narrow legs and had glowing red eyes. On its back were huge insect-like wings. "It's a Moth Man!" yelled Jack. The Moth Man opened up its mouth, there were pincher surrounding his jaws and it said, "Hummanns, you must climb hole down to escapppee." The castaways looked on in shock as the creature outside continued clawing through the window. "Who are you?" asked Max. "My nammme is Eattthhann Whittee," the Moth Man replied.

Chapter 10

The castaways stared at each other, unsure how to proceed. They stood above the pit. "Muusst gooo," said the Moth Man. "Go down Hummanns, go!" The castaways looked at the growing hole in the wall where the claw was scraping. They hurried into the pit. Max was last to go. "Hurryy, beffoore itss in!"

Max turned and looked at the Moth Man, "I want to know who the natives are? Why are they attacking us?"

"Yooou knowww alreeeadyy. Reeead bookkk."

"Do you mean your journal?" Max replied.

"Nooooo, yooourr booook. Hummmm." Max began to climb down the hole into the darkness. He wondered whether the Moth Man that was once Dr. Ethan White meant what he thought it did. Max realized that had to be the answer. The natives were the Atlanteans.

Back at the camp on the beach, Max had left the manuscript for his novel. In his book, he had given the reasons Atlantis could be real and wrote what it could have been like to live in Atlantis. He listed several locations that Atlantis may have been. Max wondered whether Atlanteans had survived after their island sank. Maybe they came to this very island. He thought back to Dr. White's journal. It had mentioned crystals. Some legends said that the Atlanteans had energy crystals. There was only one way to find out the truth.

The castaways followed the tunnel with the Moth Man pushing them on. Around a slight bend, they saw a light. "Gooooo Hummmmanns," ordered the Moth Man. They were almost out.

"I think we should head back to the camp!" yelled Max.

The cave people dragged Phillip down the path by his legs. They were leading him down the bridge, into a huge lava rock castle. He looked up and saw the gates to the castle opening. Inside, he could see only darkness. They dragged him into the darkness and for a few minutes, he could see nothing. Then, he was blinded as a bright light entered the hallway. He was dragged a few more feet before his captors stopped. His eyes slowly adjusted to the strange light and he saw he was in a large room. He heard a deep voice straight ahead of him. "So you are the one who has invaded my land!" Phillip looked up to see who had spoken.

Chapter 11

He was tall and thin with long, almost claw-like fingernails. He wore a black robe and a glowing amber crystal amulet. His face was slender with high boney cheeks. He had a goatee and his eyes were like a snake's eyes, shifting back and forth, observing all. On his forehead was a dark crown with glowing emeralds. "How many of you are there?" he commanded in a deep voice. "Why have you come to my island?"

Phillip answered, "Our plane crashed. We were stranded here, it was not our choice!"

"Liar!" he yelled. "Get the others," he said to the guards and then repeated it in a strange language.

Max, Timmy, Alice, Jack, Martha, Ruffus, and the two flight attendants walked back onto the beach. They looked around and found the camp in ruins. It was completely demolished. "Who did this?" Alice said.

Max ran to where he had slept in the camp and found his book. Just then, he heard Timmy yell, "Look at this!"

Everyone gathered around. In the sand was a briefcase and $100 bills were falling out onto the sand. "Whose is this?" Max asked.

Alice replied, "I remember hearing about a bank robbery near the airport a few days before our plane took off. It was in the news!"

Martha replied, "No one carries around a briefcase with millions of dollars inside unless they're a thief."

Max said, "It could have been one of the people the Atlanteans captured. I doubt it's one of us."

Timmy asked, "Did you say Atlanteans?"

The captured castaways stood in the center of the room. Mark, Phillip, Randon, Robert, Joe, and a flight attendant named Maria stared at the man in the robe as his crown glowed. "Why have you come to my island? Have you come to ruin my plans?"

Robert replied, "Our plane crashed in the ocean and we ended up here! Let us go, we mean no harm!"

"You are liars and if you won't tell me the truth, I'll find someone who will," replied the crowned man. He looked towards a guard and said something in the language they couldn't understand. He looked at the castaways and said, "We will release the wolves!"

Chapter 12

The ferocious pack of blood-thirsty wolves raced through the jungle. They had not left the caverns for years but maneuvered through the trees like they knew them well. They followed the scent of their prey as the full moon shined above them. They would be there soon.

The castaways argued about what to do next by the fire. They couldn't rebuild the fire on the mountain, it was too dangerous. They also didn't want to stay at their camp on the beach. The Atlanteans, if the natives were in fact Atlanteans, knew where they were. They couldn't leave the island either. The other castaways might still be alive.

Alarmingly, the bushes began to rustle. Alice grabbed a torch and lit it. She held it out towards the jungle. Eyes reflected in the firelight. Not one set of eyes, but three. Max saw them and yelled, "Run!" as three creatures burst out of the trees. The creatures were the size of dogs but had no fur and spikes running down their backs.

Someone yelled, "They're Chupacabras, run everyone!" The castaways ran down the beach. Max threw a stick at one of them.

He looked ahead and saw lights again. "It's a trap everyone, go into the jungle, it's a trap!"

The next morning, the castaways trekked through the hot and humid jungle, tired and hungry. "I think we've lost them," said Jack, "I haven't seen or heard them for over an hour."

"We have to get off this island," said one of the flight attendants.

"We have to find the others!" said Max. Just then, Max realized where they were.

"Stop!" he yelled; "This is the edge of the canyon where Phillip and Mark disappeared."

"Are you sure?" Jack asked.

"Yes, they disappeared in a cave down there," Max pointed.

"We should go. Didn't you say a flying monster attacked you here?" said the flight attendant.

"Wait," said Jack, "we haven't seen anywhere these Atlanteans could live. Phillip and Mark disappeared in a cave. Back at the steel laboratory, we went through an underground tunnel. Maybe the Atlanteans live underground?"

"You may be right," Max replied. "The cave in the canyon could be an entrance to their home. We have to go down there and save the others."

"No," said the flight attendant. "I think we should…." She was interrupted by a loud screech!

"It's the monster!" Alice yelled. "Get to cover!" The castaways ran towards the cave.

Chapter 13

The castaways ran for the cave at top speed. Max ran across the sandy ground of the canyon as the shadow of the enormous bird beast covered him in darkness. He tripped and fell to the ground, then looked up to see the talons of the bird. He jumped out of the way, but the talons grabbed Timmy. He screamed, "Help!" as the creature carried him to a giant nest on the mountainside. Max watched Timmy and the enormous bird with fear in his eyes.

Jack cried, "Get everyone into the cave immediately, I'll save Timmy!"

Jack turned around and told everyone to start moving again while Max ran towards the nest. He began to climb the wall, putting his hands and feet into holes on the cliff face, slowly moving toward the nest. Jack sighed and shook his head. The huge bird circled the mountain. Max climbed onto a rock jutting out of the cliff with just enough room for about two people. He still had about fifteen feet to go. The bird swooped down toward the nest. "Timmy, jump, I'll catch you!" Max yelled.

Timmy jumped just before the bird landed in its nest. Max grabbed his arm and pulled him onto the ledge. The giant bird beast looked down at them and let out a deafening screech. "Climb down!" Max said to Timmy. Suddenly, the rocks beneath his feet gave way and Max was left holding onto the cliff with one hand. Timmy made it to the ground and ran for the cave. Max was stuck dangling in the air. The bird beast circled around towards Max, ready to attack.

As the bird flew at him with its mouth open in a terrifying screech, Max looked down at the ground, nearly three stories below... and let go. Max tried to slow his fall by grabbing at the mountainside in his descent. He landed in a small dying bush. He had skinned his hands, knees, and hurt his leg badly, but he had survived the fall. He got up and limped toward the cave. The bird slammed against the rocky wall and was momentarily stunned. It flapped its wings several times and fell to the ground.

Max made his way painfully to the cave as the bird shook the dirt off itself and looked for its prey. He limped to the cave as the other castaways called for him to hurry. Max hobbled to the cave with all the speed he could muster as the bird slammed against the wall above him. He had made it. The castaways jumped back, as huge boulders fell over the cave entrance, sealing them all in. Dust flew up as the boulders hit the ground.

As the dust settled Max, Alice, Timmy, Jack, Martha, Ruffus, and the two flight attendants looked at the solid wall of rocks. They were trapped but safe. "Quickly, we need to start moving these rocks," said a flight attendant.

"That could take days and it's not safe!" said Alice.

Max said, "The only way out is through the cave. We have to go deeper into the tunnels, it is the only chance we have. Everyone follow me." Max led the others through the dark tunnels.

Chapter 14

As they progressed slowly through the tunnels, they entered an area with glowing crystals. Max pulled one of the glowing crystals off the wall. It was a beam of light and would light their way. The cave roof began to get lower and the passage narrowed. Suddenly, they heard footsteps. Max covered the light and whispered, "Stop! Don't move." The footsteps got louder as they came closer to the castaways, who hid behind a large stalagmite holding their breaths with apprehension. Alice looked down at her watch and noticed that her watch was no longer working. It flickered on and off. She looked at a crystal on the wall and realized it was somehow interfering with the battery. A second later the approaching footsteps stopped and turned right down another tunnel.

"Hurry, let's move," whispered Max. They continued to make their way through the tunnel, not knowing what was waiting for them in the darkness ahead.

The Moth Man stood in the shadows of the jungle near his lab. "SSSSStupiddd Hummanns, Hmmm, hmmm, hmmm, dooo not knowww hmmm, hummm, caves baaaad, hmmm, stayyy away frommm caveeee, hmmm, theeee cryteeelllss, hmmmm, theyyy doooo not knowwww truthhhh abouttt, hmmm, hmmmm, hummm, crysteeellls, hummannss!"

Max thought about his book as he led the castaways through the dark cavern, now at a slope deeper into the earth. Atlantis had sunk thousands of years ago. How could there still be Atlanteans alive today? What were these crystals that seemed to be connected to everything that was happening on the island? He was jolted from his thoughts by a scream from one of the castaways named Martha. A group of Atlanteans had appeared in front of them. Light shined from the crystals on their headbands. "Uh-oh!" Max said as the tunnel was filled with more and more Atlanteans.

Chapter 15

Max sat on the ground shoulder to shoulder with Jack and a flight attendant. They were inside of a wooden cage with wheels being pulled by a bear-like scorpion creature. The Atlanteans followed from behind. "I told you this was a bad idea," whispered the flight attendant.

"We can still escape," said Alice.

"Where do you think they're taking us?" asked Jack.

"I don't know but hopefully to the other castaways," whispered Max. The cage hit a bump and nearly tipped over. Jack yelled as it slammed back onto two wheels. An Atlantean poked Jack with the tip of his spear.

Max looked ahead and thought he saw light. "Is this the end of the tunnel? Are they bringing us into the jungle?" he said. As the light got closer and brighter, the Atlanteans looked down as if their eyes were in pain from the light. The cage stopped and the doors were opened. The Atlanteans pointed their spears and gestured for Max and the others to get up. They did and were pulled out of the cage. The Atlanteans pushed them towards the light, forcing them to walk. As they did so, Max began to see where they were heading. It wasn't the jungle.

Phillip and the other castaways were sitting on the floor of the room tied up and facing the man in the crown and robe. He had been sitting on his throne silently for over an hour. "What is he doing?" Phillip said to himself. He wondered where the other castaways were, and if the Atlanteans had left them behind on the island. His questions were answered when the doors to the room were opened and several castaways and a dog in a wooden cage were wheeled in. The man sitting in the throne rose up and said, "Finally, I have captured all you! Now, nothing can stop my plan."

Chapter 16

"Who are you? What are you talking about?!" Max yelled.

The man looked at him and replied, "I am the king of Atlantis, foolish outsiders!"

The castaways who had been in the caves looked shocked. Randon said, "Atlantis sunk thousands of years ago."

The Atlantean king looked at the castaways and angrily sneered, "Atlantis sank, but its people did not. Thousands of years ago, my people discovered the magical crystals we used could, if positioned correctly, be used as a powerful weapon. Unfortunately, our enemies attacked and turned the crystal against us, sinking our island. But we survived. My ancestors sailed from Atlantis to a nearby island where the crystals were formed once again. Our enemies continued to search for us so we hide in the lava tubes made by the island's volcano."

He continued, "We built a new Atlantis beneath the island. Eventually, our enemies gave up searching for us, but every so often someone would find our island, like the pirates that taught my great-grandfather English or that strange scientist who tried to learn the secrets of our crystals. We stopped them all. But now, we will have our revenge against the outside world. The stars and planets have aligned in such a way that it is possible to build the weapon once more! But you already know that, don't you?"

Captain Robert replied to the Atlantean king, "No, we did not know that. We are trapped on this island! Our plane crashed!"

The king of Atlantis slowly spoke, "Maybe this plane you speak of is real and maybe you are trapped, but now that you know the truth, you may never leave." The guards advanced towards the castaways when suddenly the doors to the room were thrown open. An Atlantean guard ran in quickly yelling something in their native language. The guards ran towards the door. "No!" the King yelled, "We must start the machine before they destroy it!"

He ran through a door, deeper into the castle. The sound of a loud and horrible roar echoed through the tunnels. "Everyone, try to untie yourself!" yelled Captain Robert. Frantically, the castaways attempted to untie the ropes binding their hands together.

"I just want to say I was right about the castaways being in the cave, and about the Atlanteans," said Max.

"You also got us captured," said one of the flight attendants.

"We're fine now," replied Max.

"Done!" Jack yelled, as he stood up holding his untied rope.

"Help me," said Randon. Jack hesitated, looking at the exit and back at Randon. He then bent down to help Randon. After a few minutes, everyone was untied.

"What do we do now?" Phillip asked the Captain.

"We have to find a way out of here. When I was dragged in, I saw a dock. There may be a way off this island."

"Wait!" Max yelled, "What about the weapon the king was talking about?"

Captain Robert looked at the castaways and said, "We'll have to split up. Anyone who wants to follow Max, go with him. We meet back together in an hour."

"How do we find you?" Mark asked.

"Look for the dock," replied the Captain.

Max, Mark, Randon, and Phillip went to find the king. "Good luck," yelled Jack. Alice got Ruffus out of the cage and put his leash on. As Max and the others walked down the hall, he heard Captain Robert yell back to them, "See you in an hour."

Chapter 17

Max and the others ran down the dark halls of the lava rock castle. "I think he went this way," Mark said, as they came to a bridge connecting two of the castle's towers. They heard loud yelling and saw several Atlanteans running down a bridge below.

"Look, there he is!" Randon yelled.

Max looked to where Randon was pointing and saw the king running towards a tunnel leading out of the castle's lava-filled cavern. "After him!" Max yelled. They ran, only to be startled by an inhuman roar.

Meanwhile, Captain Robert led the castaways through the dark cavern, carrying a crystal as a torch. He whispered, "Hide" as several Atlanteans ran down the tunnel past them. After they passed, the castaways resumed walking. Captain Robert looked down and was shocked to see several huge spiders crawling down the tunnel towards the sounds ahead. He wondered why there were not running away from the bizarre noises as most animals would.

The hunter did not like being underground. It preferred the shadows of the jungle to those of the caves. One of the huge cave beasts ran at it. The hunter pounced on the cave beast, dodging the sharp pointed tail. The hunter roared as it ran at another of the beasts and clawed its side.

The Moth Man flew through the caverns, followed by its spiders. "SSSSavve hummannsss, hmmm, hmmm, Stoppp Attlanntiannss, Stuppid Attllanntiaannnss, turrnnn himmm, hmmm, hmmm, innto thissssss. Failll experimmmenntts. Nowww heeeesss ledddd beaassstttt intooo caveeeee. Ledd Pannntttherrr intooo, caveeee, hmmmm, nowwww savvveee hummaaannsss.

Max led Mark, Randon, and Phillip through the tunnel. There was a bright light ahead. They had been following this tunnel upward for over twenty minutes. Max knew they didn't have much time before they had to meet up with the others. Time was running out. Max realized by now they must be near the surface. He continued to run with the others to the sunlight as the tunnel began to change from lava rock to a sandier rock mixed with dirt. He ran through the tunnel's exit into the sun and stopped, realizing they were on a mountain edge, on a platform over a huge pit. Max looked up and saw that a huge, steel machine was holding one enormous crystal. It reflected the light of the sun, directly overhead, which made looking at it nearly unbearable. Max saw on the highest platform was the King of the Atlanteans, about to pull a massive lever!

Chapter 18

"Hey King, over here!" Max yelled.

"You cannot stop me, outsiders. I will have my revenge!"

Max ran to the ladder and started to climb as the King of Atlantis pulled the lever! Max yelled down to Mark, Randon, and Phillip, "Try to slow it down, I'll go for the lever!" He scrambled towards the King and tried to grab the lever. The Atlantean King pushed him back, nearly knocking him off the platform. The crystal began to spin, first slowly, then faster. Mark, Phillip, and Randon were throwing things into the gears to slow it down, but nothing worked.

The King stood in front of the crystal and said, "If you want to stop this, you must go through me!"

Max swung at the King but missed and jumped back as the king slashed at him with his long, claw-like fingers. The crystal began to grow brighter and brighter and a loud buzzing could be heard. The King slashed at Max again, nearly hitting him. Max kicked at the Atlantean but he dodged and Max fell over off the platform. He grabbed the edge just in time. The crystal was now a glowing blur and the air filled with static. "Now, I will get my revenge once and for all."

The King lifted his foot to kick Max off the platform when a flying bottle hit his face. "Shamfroo!" Max heard Randon yell below.

The king screamed, "My eye, my eyes! What kind of a weapon is this! My eyes!" The king fell onto the platform.

Max pulled himself up and grabbed the lever, shutting down the machine. The crystal began to slow down and the buzzing became quieter. Max looked at the crystal and realized it was melting. He thought back to Dr. White's journal and yelled, "Run!" The machine cracked and buckled as the super-heated crystal melted. Max and the others ran away from the machine as liquid crystal oozed over it. They ran down the tunnel as fast as they could.

"They have ten minutes," Captain Robert said, "If they're not here by then, we'll have to leave them." They discovered that one of the tunnels exited into a large cavern connected to the ocean. They were on a dock directly below a cliff overlooking the sea. There were dozens of boats. They looked like wooden Greek battleships of the ancient past. The boats had sails, paddles jutting out of holes in the sides, and bows shaped like dragons heads. Captain Robert looked back towards the tunnels, "Ten minutes!"

Max, Randon, Mark, and Phillip ran down the tunnel. They heard yelling all around them. "I can smell saltwater!" Mark said. "It's this way!" They turned down another tunnel and ran towards the smell of the ocean.

Max saw a light up ahead. "There it is!" Max yelled. They ran towards the light and out of the tunnels. Max suddenly stopped, waving his arms back and forth. He stepped back to avoid falling. Max and the others were on top of a cliff directly over the ocean. Max looked down and saw a boat sailing out from under the cliff. They realized it was the other castaways.

"What do we do?" Phillip asked.

Mark asked, "How many feet do you think that is?"

"It's too far to jump?" said Randon.

Mark replied, "The water looks deep enough, and it's our only chance."

Max looked at Phillip and said, "There's not enough time to find another way." He looked at Randon, Mark, and Phillip and said, "Okay, on three, we jump…. one, two, three!"

Chapter 19

They plummeted into the cool water with a huge splash. Phillip opened his eyes as he sank deeper into the water. He kicked and swam to the surface. Mark, Randon, and Max all followed him. Phillip began to scream to the boat leaving the area. On the boat, Jack heard them and yelled to Captain Robert, "There they are, let's turn back and get them!"

Captain Robert turned the boat around. Co-pilot Joe threw a rope towards them. The boat neared them as Max and the others swam towards it. Joe lowered a rope ladder and they climbed aboard one after another. Joe asked, "What happened to you guys?" as the boat turned away from the terrible island. Just then, they heard a loud roar. Looking back, they saw Moth Man and the panther with the huge claws looking out of the tunnel. The Moth Man, or Dr. Ethan White, waved at them goodbye.

The boat began to move away when Ruffus ran to the side of the boat and began to bark. Alice said, "What it is now, Ruffus?"

They peered over the side of the boat and saw a large serpentine creature maneuvering through the water towards them. It dived under the water, leaving a large ripple. "What is that thing?" said Captain Robert from the deck.

Something hit the bottom of the boat, knocking Captain Robert and a suitcase across the deck. Ruffus yelped and hid under Alice. Max ran towards the edge of the boat as the huge serpent flew out of the water. The castaways shuddered in fear as they saw a scaly dark green neck rising over the boat. Looming over them was the head of the serpent. It had snake-like eyes, jagged spiked teeth, a dragon like skull, and sharp spines running down its back. It had a horn on its nose and it was a slimy olive color.

The serpent suddenly opened its mouth and spoke, "You destroyed my machine and crystal but I will have my revenge." Max knew it was the King of Atlantis. The crystals mutated him when they had melted. The serpent slammed its head into the boat, ripping a hole through the deck. Max ran from the King as he tried to snatch him with his sharp jagged teeth.

Joe yelled, "Get below deck everyone, there are cannons!"

The King roared, "You cannot stop my revenge!" There was an explosion as a cannonball tore into the King's stomach. It jerked back as more were fired and it wailed in anger. A final shot hit the Serpent King in the jaw, and the Serpent King dived underwater. Max ran towards the edge of the boat and saw the Serpent King swimming towards them once again.

The Moth Man yelled from the cave and the panther with its massive claws hurled a huge lava rock at the serpent. The rock landed on the Serpent King's back and pushed him down deep to the ocean floor. Captain Robert and the others turned the boat so they could flee as quickly as possible. They sailed away and the Serpent King didn't follow. They were finally leaving the Island of the Monsters. The flight attendant peered at Captain Robert and asked, "What's in the briefcase, Captain?" Max walked over to the Captain and noticed money in all his pockets.

Epilogue

The castaways sailed for several days before being discovered by a cruise ship. When the cruise pulled up, Captain Robert was tied to the mast.

Max's manuscript was lost on the island but he rewrote it as an adventure story about the island. It sold millions of copies all over the world.

Jack climbed Mt. Fuji and after that Mt. Everest.

Alice won the lottery and Ruffus got lots of chew toys.

Randon sold his Shamfroo as a riot control weapon.

Timmy was reunited with his family and won the spelling bee.

Captain Robert was sent to prison for armed robbery and impersonating a pilot.

The Moth Man, aka. Dr. Ethan White, became king of the island.

About the Author

Noah F. Bunyan is 14 years-old and lives in Okinawa, Japan with his Mom, sister Maria, dog Luna, and cats Chester and Smoky Jan Jones. Noah has been writing since he was six and has published five Lightning Man graphic novels. Noah has lived in Germany, Guantanamo Bay Cuba, Italy, and Okinawa in Japan. He is a ninth grade student at DoDDS Kubasaki High School.

Noah would like to thank his mother and sister for all their help and encouragement. Noah enjoys writing, illustrating, and reading.

Made in the USA
Las Vegas, NV
12 October 2021